Disney · PIXAR

INCREDIBLES 2

BABYSITTING MODE

By Sarah Hernandez

Illustrated by the Disney Storybook Art Team

A Random House PICTUREBACK® Book

Random House 🏠 New York

Copyright © 2018 Disney Enterprises, Inc. and Pixar.
All right reserved. Published in the United States by Random House Children's Books, a division of Penguin Random House LLC,
1745 Broadway, New York, NY 10019, and in Canada by Penguin Random House Canada Limited, Toronto, in conjunction with Disney
Enterprises, Inc. Pictureback, Random House, and the Random House colophon are trademarks of Penguin Random House LLC.
rhcbooks.com
ISBN 978-0-525-58159-8
Printed in the United States of America
10 9 8 7 6 5 4 3 2 1

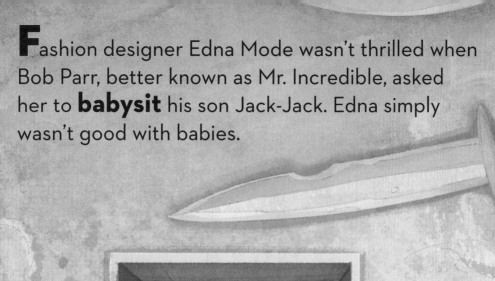

Fashion designer Edna Mode wasn't thrilled when Bob Parr, better known as Mr. Incredible, asked her to **babysit** his son Jack-Jack. Edna simply wasn't good with babies.

But Jack-Jack was no *ordinary* baby. As soon as his dad left, Jack-Jack began to float! Edna was delighted, and she wondered what else he could do.

Edna knew that each Super was unique . . . but there was something **extra special** about little Jack-Jack.

She wanted to observe him and take notes for his next Supersuit design. Where was her sketchbook? There was no time to find it—Jack-Jack was **on the move**!

Edna was thrilled to see Jack-Jack **walk right through a wall**.

You are amazing, *dahling!*

The little boy couldn't
be **stopped**!

He continued to phase **in and out** of the
walls as he floated down the hallway.

Suddenly, Jack-Jack **disappeared**!
Where in the world can that little boy be? Edna
wondered as she searched. *I simply must put a*
tracking device *in his next Supersuit.*

Come out,
come out,
dahling.

Finally, Edna found Jack-Jack downstairs, near her lab. The Super baby smiled and pointed at his **new discovery . . .**

. . . flashing lights on a wall!
Jack-Jack had found the security system for Edna's testing room! The alarm began to beep.
In the blink of an eye, Jack-Jack **morphed** into a pint-sized Edna. The alarm stopped!

Edna Mode.
ACCESS GRANTED.

Edna marveled at the miniature version of herself. She had never seen anything so **extraordinary**.

Inside, little Jack-Jack discovered some of the Supersuits Edna had designed. He **couldn't wait** to get his hands on the colorful costumes.

Jack-Jack tried on bits and pieces of many different costumes. He even fashioned a cape for himself. But Edna shared her **one and only** design rule.

Jack-Jack loved the cape he had created and didn't want to take it off. He got so **angry** that he turned into a little monster! Edna didn't panic—she was used to working with Supers of all kinds.

Edna knew it was time for Jack-Jack's bottle.
But how would she calm him down long enough
to feed him? She wondered if **music** would help
Jack-Jack change back into a baby.

Edna played Beethoven for the little monster. **It worked!** He transformed back into an adorable baby.

But suddenly, **ONE** Jack-Jack multiplied into **TWO** . . .

... THREE ... FOUR ...
FIVE Jack-Jacks!

There was no way
Edna could feed five
hungry Jack-Jacks
with just one bottle!

Edna switched the music to Mozart. **Success!** All the Jack-Jacks merged into one baby. He began to giggle as he watched his bottle heat up on the stove, and then . . .

... WHOOOOSH! Jack-Jack **burst into flames**!

Edna remained calm—**she had seen it ALL**.

After putting out Jack-Jack's flames, Edna finally **spotted** her sketchbook.

But it was hard to design a
Supersuit for Jack-Jack when he kept
destroying her pencils with his
laser-beam eyes!
She tried to keep him busy with his bottle.

Later that evening, Edna told Jack-Jack a story about the **adventures** of his family, the Incredibles, and their heroic little boy—who, of course, used his amazing powers to **save the day**!